DiPPY

THE NATION'S FAVOURITE DINOSAUR

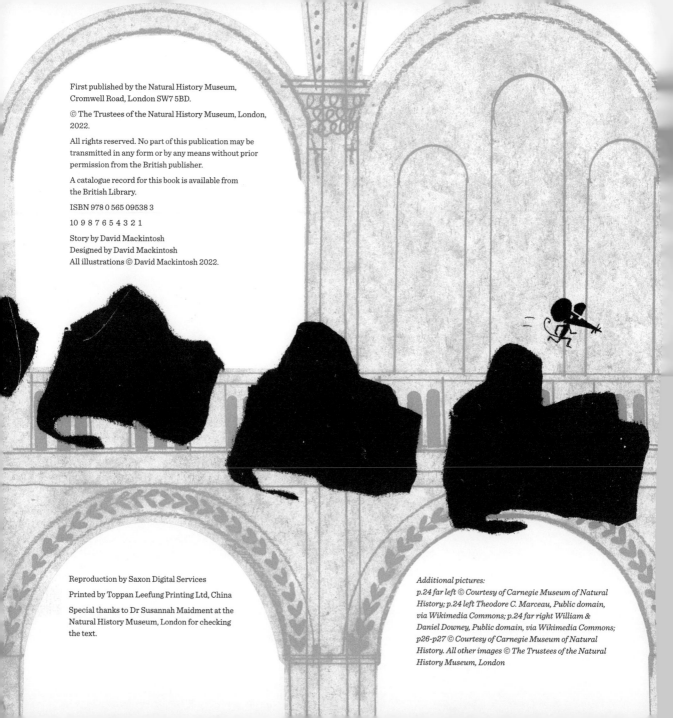

First published by the Natural History Museum,
Cromwell Road, London SW7 5BD.

© The Trustees of the Natural History Museum, London,
2022.

A catalogue record for this book is available from
the British Library.

ISBN 978 0 565 09538 3

10 9 8 7 6 5 4 3 2 1

Story by David Mackintosh
Designed by David Mackintosh
All illustrations © David Mackintosh 2022

Reproduction by Saxon Digital Services

Printed by Toppan Leefung Printing Ltd, China

Special thanks to Dr Susannah Maidment at the
Natural History Museum, London for checking
the text.

Additional pictures:
p.24 far left © Courtesy of Carnegie Museum of Natural
History; p.24 left Theodore C. Marceau, Public domain,
via Wikimedia Commons; p.24 far right William &
Daniel Downey, Public domain, via Wikimedia Commons;
p26-p27 © Courtesy of Carnegie Museum of Natural
History. All other images © The Trustees of the Natural
History Museum, London

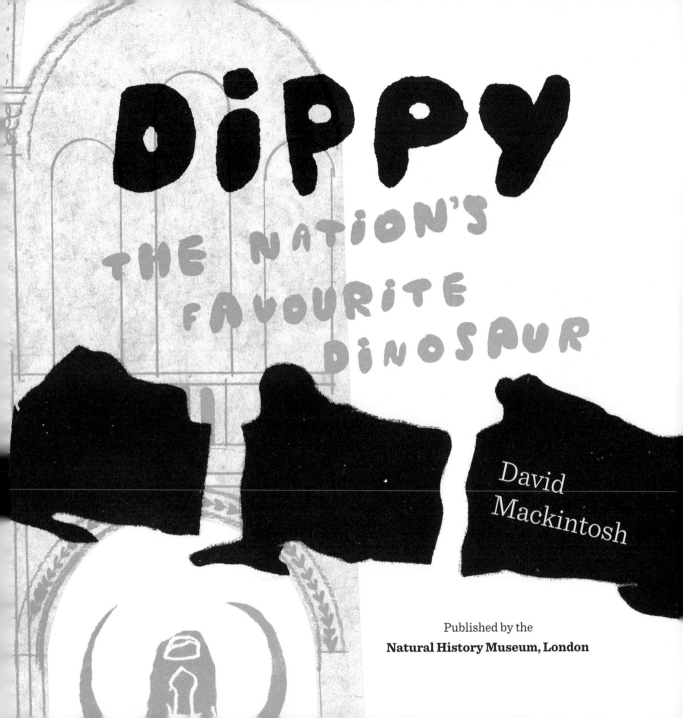

Dippy

THE NATION'S FAVOURITE DINOSAUR

David
Mackintosh

Published by the
Natural History Museum, London

One day, emerging from a hole in the wall, Waterhouse noticed something different about the Museum.

A **gigantic** skeleton had appeared – a skeleton *bigger than any seen before*. It towered above the floor – and it towered above Waterhouse.

The little mouse knew each and every object in the Natural History Museum by name – but this was a mystery.

PRIVATE: no public access

Waterhouse
wanted some
answers...

At that moment, a booming voice
echoed around the Museum –
a voice as big as the skeleton itself.

" *Dippy is a* **Diplodocus** *and*
belongs to a group of dinosaurs known as
sauropods, *meaning 'lizard feet'.*
All sauropods have a very small head, extremely
long neck, a body shaped like a barrel, legs like
pillars and a long slender tail. **"**

Waterhouse found this *very* interesting.

But the little mouse wanted to know *more*
about this bony stranger...

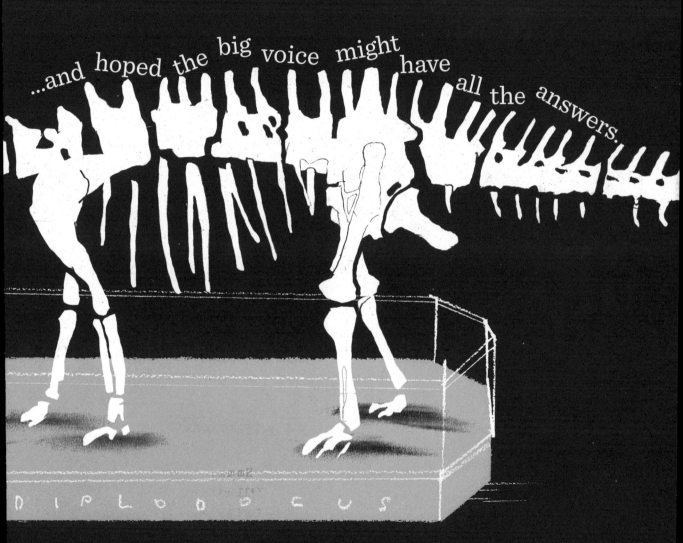

How do you say Diplodocus?

" *Well, there are many different ways to say Diplodocus. I think that when you say it out loud it should sound like...*

'dip-LOW-dock-US',

with the emphasis on the 'dip' *and the* 'dock'.

But some people prefer to say

'dip-low-doe-cus',

or sometimes even

'dip-LOD-oh-CUS'. "

Hmmm... I'll stick to Dippy.

Waterhouse asked another.

What does Diplodocus mean?

" DIPLODOCUS means 'double-beam' from the Greek words **diplos**, meaning double, and **dokos**, meaning beam. "

25 26 27

" It is called this because some of the bones in its tail have two branches...

one pointing forward and one pointing backward.

Most other reptiles have a single backward-pointing bone. "

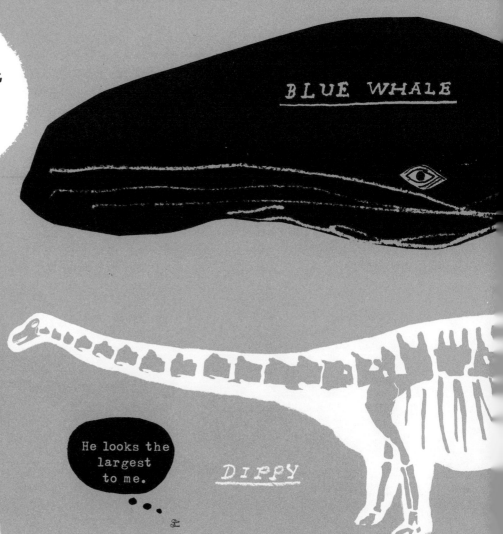

Is Dippy the largest dinosaur ever?

BLUE WHALE

66 *Sauropods are the largest land animals ever known and even though Diplodocus is not the largest, it is one of the longest. Dippy is 26 metres or 85 feet long.* 99

He looks the largest to me.

DIPPY

1 2 3 4 5 6 7 8 9 10 11 12 13

Does Dippy have the same number of bones and teeth as me?

" Including all the bones in its head, Dippy has 356 bones and 46 teeth. Adult humans have 206 bones and 32 teeth. "

" Oh...and mice have slightly more bones than humans and half the number of teeth.
Got it? "

15 16 17 18 19 20 21 22 23 24 25 26

* Dippy is almost as tall as a red London bus, and twice as tall as the front door of the Museum

Where and when did Dippy live?

66 *Diplodocus fossils have only been found in Colorado, Montana, New Mexico, Utah and Wyoming, which are all in North America. None have been found anywhere else in the world. Scientists think that Diplodocus lived there between 156 and 145 million years ago, when the land was covered in rivers and forests. They probably travelled around together in herds, like elephants do today.* 99

ARCTIC OCEAN

NORTH SEA

EURO[PE]

H[A]ICA

NORTH ATLANTIC OCEAN

New York

NATURAL HISTORY MUSEUM, LONDON.

[GU]LF of [M]EXICO

AF[RICA]

CARIBBEAN SEA

SOUTH AMERICA

SOUTH ATLANTIC OCEAN

Why did Dippy have such a long neck?

" Dippy could move its neck both from side-to-side and up-and-down. When Dippy was alive there were lots of plant-eating animals competing for food. So, by having such a long neck, Dippy could reach nourishing leaves high in the tree tops and bushes and trees each side of it that other animals couldn't. "

What did Dippy use its tail for?

66 *Dippy had a very long tail and may have used it like a whip to defend itself against meat-eating dinosaurs, like Allosaurus. Its tail may also have helped it to keep its balance when it stretched out its long neck for food, or reared up on its back legs to reach up high.* **99**

Where was Dippy's nose?

" Dippy's nose was right between its eyes, almost at the top of its head.

This made scientists think that Diplodocus lived in water and used its long neck like a snorkel to breathe, with just its nostrils out of the water. "

" Maybe having its nostrils between its eyes protected them when it pushed its snout into trees and bushes. "

" Now however, most scientists agree that Diplodocus lived mainly on land. "

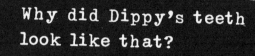

Why did Dippy's teeth look like that?

" Dippy had rows of pencil-like teeth, like a comb, bunched together at the front of its mouth. Scientists think it used this comb to strip leaves from the branches and then swallowed them straight away, without chewing! "

No wonder it's extinct, thought Waterhouse.

What did Dippy eat?

" Probably not what you'd expect! Dippy was a plant eater and ate hundreds of kilograms of leaves and other vegetation every day to provide energy to support its enormous body. "

Oh! So Dippy was vegetarian?

Of course, Waterhouse had *tons* of questions about Dippy.

Was Dippy a male or a female?

" *We don't know. It's very difficult to tell the sex of a dinosaur. And although Dippy's skeleton was almost complete, some bones came from other dinosaur fossils, and so Dippy may be a mix of male and female.* "

How old was Dippy when it died?

66 *We can't tell from the fossil bones how old Dippy was when it died but we do think it was a fully grown adult. Diplodocus are thought to have lived for up to 70 years, about the age an elephant lives to today.* 99

There is certainly more to Dippy than meets the eye! thought Waterhouse, slowly absorbing all the Dippy facts.

But one question Waterhouse wanted answered was not about how Dippy lived, where it was from or even what it ate. It was simpler than that...

Just HOW did Dippy come to be here at the Museum?

With a deep breath, the big voice replied:

" *I thought you'd never ask...*

THE NATURAL HISTORY MUSEUM

1902

how splendid!

WYOMING, AMERICA

1898

how much?

Andrew Carnegie

"
Dippy was discovered in 1898 in Wyoming, America. It was unearthed from where it had lain for millions of years.

When Andrew Carnegie – then one of the world's richest men – heard about the fossil he decided to buy it.

In 1902 the King of England visited Andrew at his castle in Scotland and spotted a drawing of Dippy on the wall.

The King remarked how wonderful it would be to have such an animal in the Natural History Museum in London. Andrew agreed.

FRAGILE

BOX 1 OF 100

To:
NHM
LONDON

FROM:
A. CARNEGIE

HANDLE WITH CARE

THIS WAY UP

PVA

1905

LONDON, ENGLAND

Some of Dippy's bones were missing so bones from other Diplodocus fossils were used to make up a complete dinosaur.

Andrew then arranged for a copy of all the bones to be made.

The copy was then shipped from America to London, the bones put together and Dippy was put on display for all of the Museum's visitors to see in 1905. And THAT'S how Dippy came to London. 99

What happened to the original Dippy?

❝ That's a good question. The original skeleton was put on display in the Carnegie Museum of Natural History in Pittsburgh, America in 1907. Other copies were also made for Paris, Berlin, Vienna, Bologna, St. Petersburg (it is now in Moscow), La Plata, Madrid and Mexico City, and all of these are still on display. ❞

Greetings *from* PITTSBURG

ₚₑₙₙₛᵧₗᵥₐₙᵢₐ.

POST CARD

REAL PHOTOGRAPH (COPYRIGHT)

H.

Diplodocus

What a story Dippy has to tell!

But Waterhouse couldn't help thinking that such an enormous creature would rather be *outside* – in the fresh air and with a little more space. After all, Dippy might like to see the sights of London too.

In the meantime, Waterhouse was happy for Dippy to stay right where it was.

Waterhouse knew more about
Dippy now than ever before.

The mouse applauded the sauropod
for its *fascinating* story.

But Dippy just stood silently,
saying *nothing*,
like a statue.

Then a
familiar
voice echoed
around the
Museum,
one last
time...

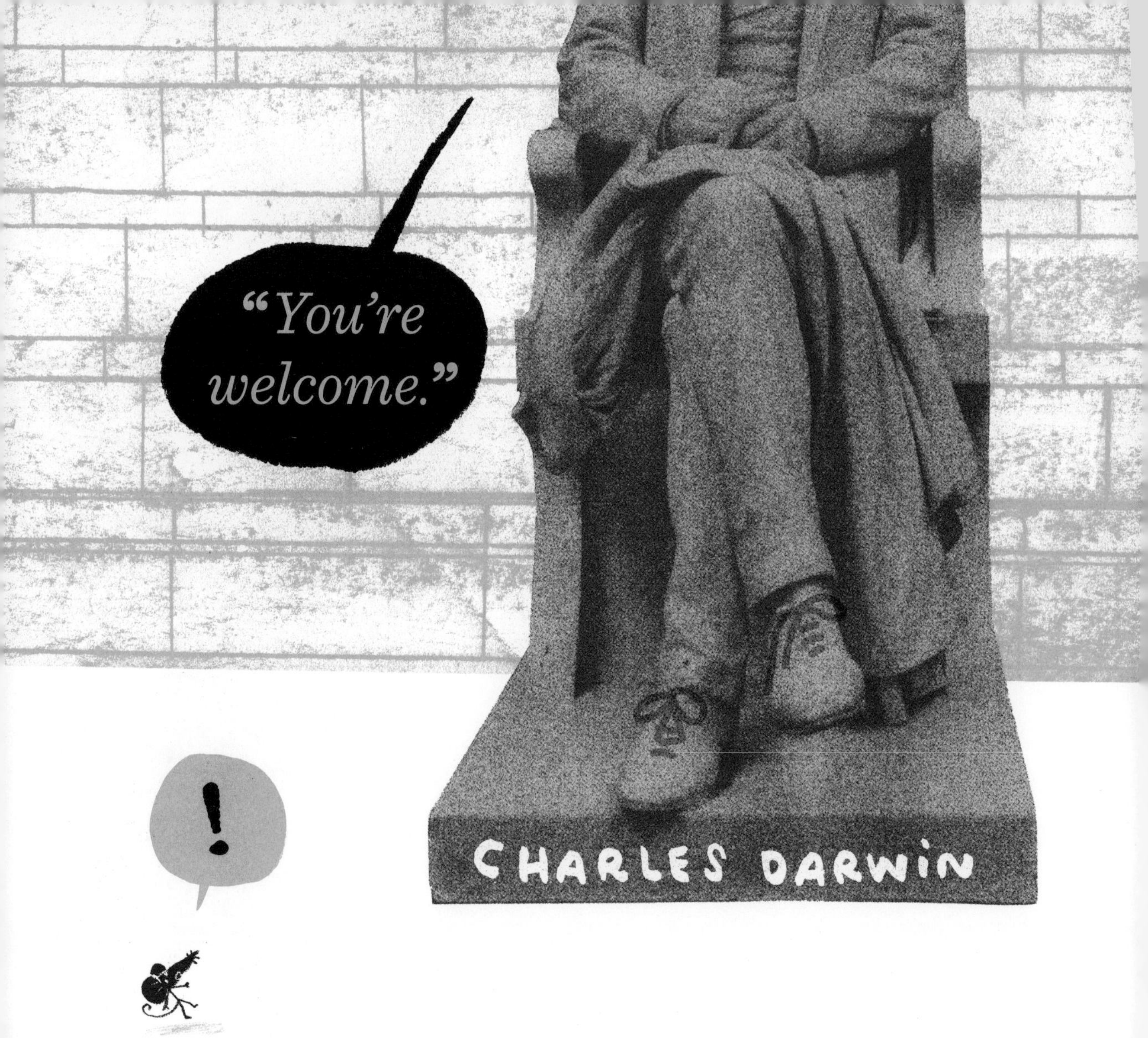
"You're welcome."
!
CHARLES DARWIN